SCHNITZEL IS LOST

SCHNITZEL IS LOST

By Hans Wilhelm

Simon & Schuster Books for Young Readers

Published by Simon & Schuster
New York • London • Toronto • Sydney • Tokyo • Singapore

 SIMON & SCHUSTER BOOKS FOR YOUNG READERS

Simon & Schuster Building, Rockefeller Center, 1230 Avenue of the Americas, New York, New York 10020

Copyright © 1991 by Hans Wilhelm, Inc. All rights reserved including the right of reproduction in whole or in part in any form.

SIMON & SCHUSTER BOOKS FOR YOUNG READERS is a trademark of Simon & Schuster

Designed by Lucille Chomowicz. Manufactured in the United States of America   10   9   8   7   6   5   4   3   2   1

Library of Congress Cataloging-in-Publication Data

Wilhelm, Hans, 1945-   Schnitzel is lost / by Hans Wilhelm.   p.   cm.   Summary: Schnitzel the dog becomes separated from his best friend Pretzel when he ventures from his back yard to chase leaves. [1. Dogs—Fiction.   2. Lost children—Fiction.   3. Friendship—Fiction.]   I. Title.   PZ7.W64816Sb   1991   [E]—dc20   90-43325   ISBN 0-671-73306-0

 *To Nurit*

One day, the garden gate was left open.

When Schnitzel saw it, he cried, "Yippie! Let's explore!"

"Wait," said his friend Pretzel. "Maybe we shouldn't. It might be dangerous."

"Don't be silly," replied Schnitzel as he raced through the gate and into the street.

Pretzel followed Schnitzel as he jumped into a huge pile of leaves. "What fun!" Schnitzel shouted, and Pretzel had to agree. It was certainly more exciting here than in their back yard.

"Let's catch leaves," suggested Schnitzel as he
followed a beautiful yellow leaf that danced in
the wind.

"Please don't go too far," cried Pretzel.

But Schnitzel did not hear. He was too busy chasing his leaf.

He ran and ran, and finally he caught it. Then he looked around. "Where am I?" he wondered. "Where are the trees …the leaves? Where is Pretzel?"

"Oh, no!" he cried.
"I hope I'm not lost!"

He ran back the way he thought he had come,

but he could find no trees. And no Pretzel.

He ran up and down, street after street, and still nothing looked like home. Finally, Schnitzel knew that he was hopelessly lost.

Tears came to Schnitzel's eyes. "I'm lost. Please help me," he cried. "I want to go home!" But it seemed that no one had time for a little lost dog.

Over and over again, Schnitzel cried, "I want to go home!"

After a while, Schnitzel knew he had to do something.
He couldn't just wait here where nobody knew him or
even cared what happened to him.

"Maybe I should try the other side of the street,"
he thought, and carefully stepped off the curb.

Screech went the tires of a huge car as it nearly ran over Schnitzel. Frightened, he ran on as fast as his legs would carry him.

Suddenly, he was no longer alone. Someone was chasing him. Someone much bigger than Schnitzel. Someone with a terrible grin and huge teeth!

No matter how fast Schnitzel ran, those huge
teeth kept getting closer and closer.

At a corner, Schnitzel saw several people going through a narrow door. Schnitzel ran for it as fast as he could. "I hope I can lose him there," he thought.

Quickly, the doors closed behind Schnitzel.
He was safe at last.
    At least, that's what he thought!

Suddenly, the whole place moved and shook! Nobody around
Schnitzel seemed to notice, but Schnitzel was frightened. "I have
to get out of here," he thought. "This is too scary."

After a while, the doors opened again and Schnitzel
jumped out as fast as he could…right into a huge pile
of leaves!

"Wow!" cried Schnitzel. "This looks like the same pile of leaves I played in with Pretzel. He looked around and saw the gate to his backyard.

It was still open! Schnitzel was *home* again!

Running up the steps, he caught a beautiful yellow leaf.

Pretzel was so happy when Schnitzel came in. "Where were you? I was so worried. What happened?" she cried.

"I was chasing leaves." said Schnitzel. "Why? Did you think I was lost?"

"Of course not." Pretzel smiled. "You are much too clever for that."

Schnitzel blushed. Then he gave Pretzel the leaf. "This is for you," he said.

"Thank you," said Pretzel. "It's beautiful."

That night, before the two friends went to sleep, Pretzel asked Schnitzel, "Were you scared when you were lost?"

"Well, a little," admitted Schnitzel, and cuddled a little closer to his friend Pretzel.